Susannah and the Sandman

A GOOD-NIGHT STORY BY
Monika Laimgruber

Translated by Marianne Martens

North-South Books / New York / London

Copyright © 1996 by Nord-Süd Verlag AG, Gossau Zürich, Switzerland.
First published in Switzerland under the title *Leontines Kopfkissenbuch*. English translation copyright © 1996 by North-South Books Inc.
First published in the United States, Great Britain, Canada, Australia, and New Zealand in 1996 by North-South Books,
an imprint of Nord-Süd Verlag AG, Gossau Zürich, Switzerland. Distributed in the United States by North-South Books Inc., New York.

For information about this and other North-South books, visit our web site at: http://www.northsouth.com
Library of Congress Cataloging-in-Publication Data is available. A CIP catalogue record for this book is available from The British Library.
ISBN 1-55858-601-6 (trade binding)   ISBN 1-55858-602-4 (library binding)
1 2 3 4 5 6 7 8 9 10 TB   Printed in Belgium   LB 10 9 8 7 6 5 4 3 2 1

Every evening when the sun goes down, the Sandman awakens.
He goes out into the world with a bag of magic sand which he sprinkles
on children to send them off to deep sleep and sweet dreams.

But tonight he has a problem: Susannah doesn't want to go to sleep. Soft, silvery moonlight shines on her bed. Everyone else is already asleep—Sara the doll, Stubby the bear, Steffi the cat, and Sam the dog. But Susannah is still awake.

Susannah stacks her pillows into a huge pile and climbs to the very top. "Who are all those sleeping monsters down below?" she cries. "I'd better attack before they wake up!"
And with that, Susannah starts throwing pillows.

The monsters are wide awake now.
As they come closer and closer, the pile
of pillows collapses, burying the
Sandman's bag.

Susannah flings pillow after pillow at the invaders,
but they throw them right back at her.
It's a pillow fight!

Everyone leaps and romps around the room,
barking, growling, and laughing.

Tired at last, Susannah snuggles under a mountain of pillows, and finally the Sandman can find his bag.

All is quiet.
Susannah sees the Sandman
sprinkling his magic sand
to send her off to sleep.

The pillows rise and float away, carrying Susannah
and all her friends.

They follow the Sandman to his magical world
of deep sleep and sweet dreams.

The next morning, warm, golden sunlight shines through
the bedroom window. Sara the doll, Stubby the bear, Steffi the cat,
and Sam the dog are all awake, but the Sandman's magic is still
working on Susannah, who's sound asleep, dreaming sweet dreams.